Marx Abbott Hardy Machiavelli Montaigne Chesterton Cooper Emerson Joyce Austen
Defoe Melville Haggard Hugo Eliot Grimm
Stoker Carroll Christie Molière Cooper
Wilde Maupassant Byron Schiller
Garnett Einstein Fitzgerald Engels Smith Kafka
Goethe Hawthorne Hall
Cotton Dostoyevsky Willis
Baum Kipling Doyle
Henry Nietzsche
Leslie Dumas Flaubert Turgenev Balzac
Stockton Vatsyayana Crane
Burroughs Verne
Curtis Tocqueville Gogol Vinci
Homer Widger Tolstoy Whitman Busch
Darwin Thoreau Twain Scott Plato Harte
Potter Freud Zola Lawrence Dickens Burton Hesse
Kant Jowett Stevenson
Andersen
London Descartes Cervantes
Poe Aristotle Wells Voltaire Cooke
Hale James Hastings Burton
Bunner Shakespeare Irving
Richter Chekhov Chambers Alcott
Doré Dante Swift da Shaw Wodehouse Benedict Pushkin Newton

The Recitation

George Herbert Betts

Imprint

This book is part of TREDITION CLASSICS

Author: George Herbert Betts
Cover design: Buchgut, Berlin – Germany

Publisher: tredition GmbH, Hamburg - Germany
ISBN: 978-3-8472-2983-4

www.tredition.com
www.tredition.de

Copyright:
The content of this book is sourced from the public domain.

The intention of the TREDITION CLASSICS series is to make world literature in the public domain available in printed format. Literary enthusiasts and organizations, such as Project Gutenberg, worldwide have scanned and digitally edited the original texts. tredition has subsequently formatted and redesigned the content into a modern reading layout. Therefore, we cannot guarantee the exact reproduction of the original format of a particular historic edition. Please also note that no modifications have been made to the spelling, therefore it may differ from the orthography used today.

THE RECITATION

BY

GEORGE HERBERT BETTS, Ph. D.

PROFESSOR OF PSYCHOLOGY

CORNELL COLLEGE, IOWA

CONTENTS

Editor's Introduction

I. The Purposes of the Recitation

II. The Method of the Recitation

III. The Art of Questioning

IV. Conditions Necessary To a Good Recitation

V. The Assignment of the Lesson

Outline

EDITOR'S INTRODUCTION

Teachers are not always clear as to what they mean when they speak of the recitation. Many different meanings are associated with the term. Some of these are suggestive but quite vague; and others, although more definite, are but partial truths that hinder as much as they help. It is not surprising that a confused usage of the term is current among teachers.

From one point of view, the recitation is a recitation-period, a segment of the daily time schedule. In this sense it is an administrative unit, valuable in apportioning to each school subject its part of the time devoted to the curriculum. Thus, we speak of five recitations in arithmetic, three in music, or two in drawing, having in mind merely the number of times the class meets for instruction in a particular school study. A recitation here means no more than a class-period, a more or less arbitrary device for controlling the teacher's and pupils' distribution of energy among the various subjects taught.

[vi]

From another point of view, the recitation is a form of educative activity rather than a mere time allotment. In this sense the recitation is a process of instruction, a mode of teaching, wherein pupils and teacher, facing a common situation, proceed toward a more or less conscious end. It is a distinct movement in classroom experience, so organized that a definite beginning, progression, and end are clearly distinguishable. Thus we speak of the method of the recitation, the five formal steps of the recitation, or the various types of recitation. Such a usage makes "recitation" synonymous with "lesson." Indeed, when we pass from general pedagogical discussion to a detailed treatment of special methods of teaching, we usually abandon the term "recitation" and use the word "lesson." Although there is always some notion of a time-period in the curriculum in our idea of a lesson, yet the term "lesson" is more intimately connected with the thought of a teaching exercise in which ideas are developed and fixed in memory. It is through the lesson or recitation that pupils and teachers influence one another's [vii]thought and action; and when this condition exists, there is always educative activity.

These two ways of thinking of the recitation, one primarily administrative and the other primarily educative, need to be somewhat sharply differentiated in our thinking. However closely related they are in actual schoolroom work, however greatly they influence each other in practice, they require a theoretic separation. Only by this method can we avoid some of the error and confusion current in teaching theory and practice. A single instance will suffice to show the value of the distinction.

No one of us would deliberately assume that the teaching process required for the instruction of a child would just cover the twenty, thirty, or forty minutes allotted to the class-period, day after day and year after year, regardless of the subject presented or the child taught. Yet this is precisely the sort of assumption that is implied throughout a considerable portion of our current discussion of the teaching process. We talk about a "developmental-lesson" or a "review-recitation" in, say, geography, as though it began [viii]and ended with the recitation-period of the day. The daily lesson-plans we demand of apprentice-teachers in training-schools are largely built upon this basis.

Of course the fact that one must begin a theme at a given moment and close at a similar arbitrary point affects the teacher's procedure somewhat. He will always have to attack the problem anew at ten o'clock and pull together the loose ends of discussion at ten-thirty, if these happen to be the limits of time assigned him. But who will be bold enough to assert that the psychological movement for the development and solution of the particular problem at hand will always be exactly thirty minutes long? It is possible, and quite probable, that the typical movements in instruction — development, drill, examination, practice, and review — may occur within a single class-period, following fast upon the heels of each other as the situation may demand. It is equally probable that in many cases any one of them may reach across several class-periods. We need a more flexible way of thinking of the recitation and of the teaching activities involved [ix]in class-periods and of other administrative factors which condition the effectiveness of teaching.

Such a clear, flexible treatment of the recitation is offered in this volume. We feel that it will be particularly welcome to the practical teacher since so many previous treatments of this subject have been formal or obscure. Combining the training of a psychologist with the experience of a class teacher, Professor Betts has given us a lucid, helpful, and common-sense treatment of the recitation without falling into scientific technicality or pedagogical formalism.

[1]

I

THE PURPOSES OF THE RECITATION

The teacher has two great functions in the school; one is that of organizing and managing, the other, that of teaching.

In the first capacity he forms the school into its proper divisions or classes, arranges the programme of daily recitations and other exercises, provides for calling and dismissing classes, passing into and out of the room, etc., and controls the conduct of the pupils; that is, keeps order.

The organization and management of the school is of the highest importance, and fundamental to everything else that goes on in the school. A large proportion of the teachers who are looked upon as unsuccessful fail at this point. Probably at least two out of three who lose their positions are dropped from inability to organize and manage a school. While this is true, how[2]ever, the organizing and managing of the school is wholly secondary; it exists only that the *teaching* may go on. Teaching is, after all, the primary thing. Lacking good teaching, no amount of good management or organization can redeem the school.

1. *The teacher and the recitation*

Teaching goes on chiefly in what we call the *recitation*. This is the teacher's point of contact with his pupils; here he meets them face to face and mind to mind; here he succeeds or fails in his function of teaching.

Failure in teaching is harder to measure than failure in organization and management. It quickly becomes noised abroad if the children are not well classified, or if the teacher cannot keep order. If the machinery of the school does not run smoothly, its creaking soon attracts public attention, and the skill of the teacher is at once called into question. But the teacher may be doing indifferent work in the recitation, and the class hardly be aware of it and the patrons know nothing about it. There is no definite measure[3] for the amount of inspiration a teacher is giving daily to his pupils, and no foot-rule with which to test the worth of his instruction in the recitation.

And it is this very fact that makes it so necessary that the teacher should study the principles of teaching as applied to the recitation. The difficulty of accurately measuring failure in actual teaching tends to make us all careless at this point. Yet this is the very point above all others that is vital to the pupil. Inspiring teaching may compensate in large degree for poor management, but nothing can make up to a pupil for dull and unskillful teaching. If the recitations are for him a failure, nothing else can make the school a success so far as he is concerned.

The ultimate measure of a teacher, therefore, is the measure taken before his class, while he is conducting a recitation.

2. *The necessity of having a clear aim*

Any discussion of the recitation should begin with its aims or purposes; for upon aim or purpose everything else depends. For example, if[4] you ask me the best method of conducting a recitation, I shall have to inquire before answering, whether your purpose in this recitation is to discover what the pupils have prepared of the work assigned them; or to introduce the class to a new subject, such as percentage in arithmetic; or to drill them, as upon the multiplication table. Each of these purposes would demand a different method in the recitation. Again, if your purpose is to show off a class before visitors, you will need to use a very different method from what you will employ if your aim is to encourage the class in self-expression and independence in thinking.

There are three great purposes to be accomplished through the recitation: *testing*, *teaching*, and *drilling*. These three aims may all be accomplished at times in the same recitation, may even alternate with each other in successive questions, but they are nevertheless wholly distinct from each other, and require different methods for their accomplishment. The skillful teacher will have one or the other of these three aims before him either consciously or unconsciously at each moment of the recitation, and will know when[5] he changes from one to the other and for what reason. Let us proceed to consider each of these aims somewhat more in detail.

3. *Testing as an aim in the recitation*

Testing deals with ground already covered, with matter already learned, or with powers already developed. It concerns itself with the old, instead of progressing into the new. It seeks to find out what the child knows or what he can do of that which he has already been over in his work. Of course every new lesson or task attempted is in some measure a test of all that has preceded it, but testing needs to be much more definite and specific than this.

The testing discussed here must not be confused with what we sometimes call "tests," but which really are examinations, given at more or less infrequent intervals. Testing may and should be carried on in the regular daily recitations by questions and answers either oral or written, bearing on matter previously assigned; by discussions of topics of the lesson assigned; or by requiring new work involving the knowledge or[6] power gained in the past work which is being tested. The following are some of the principal things which we should test in the recitation: —

a. The preparation of the lesson assigned. — The preparation of every lesson assigned should be tested in some definite way. This is of the utmost importance, especially in all elementary grades. We are all so constituted mentally that we have a tendency to grow careless in assigned tasks if their performance is not strictly required of us. No matter how careful may be the assignment of the lesson, and no matter how much the teacher may urge upon the class at the time of the assignment that they prepare the lesson well, the pupils must be held responsible for this preparation day by day, without fail, if we are to insure their mastery of it.

Nor is it enough to inquire, "How many understand this lesson?" or "How many got all the examples?" It is the teacher's business to test thoroughly for himself the pupil's mastery of the lesson or the knowledge or power required for the examples, in some definite and concrete way. It will not suffice to take the pupil's judgment[7] of his own preparation and mastery, for many will allow a hazy or doubtful point to go by unexplained rather than confess before teacher and class their lack of study or inability to grasp the topic. Further, pupils seldom have the standards of mastery which enable them to judge what constitutes an adequate grasp of the subject.

b. The pupil's knowledge and his methods of study.—Entirely aside from the question of the preparation of the lesson assigned, the teacher must constantly test the pupil's knowledge in order that he may know how and what next to teach him; for no maxim of teaching is better established than that we should proceed from the known to the related unknown. And this is only another way of saying that we should build all new knowledge upon the foundation of knowledge already mastered.

To illustrate: Pupils must have a thorough mastery and ready knowledge of addition, subtraction, multiplication, and division before we can proceed to teach them measurements or fractions. And without doubt much time is wasted in attempting to teach these subjects without a ready[8] command of the fundamental operations. Further, pupils must know well both common and decimal fractions before they can proceed to percentage. They must know and be able to recognize readily the different "parts of speech" before they can analyze sentences in grammar.

But not less important than what the pupil knows is *how* he knows the thing; that is, what are his methods of study and learning. The pupil in a history class may be able to recite whole pages of the text almost verbatim, but when questioned as to the meaning of the events and facts show very little knowledge about them. A student confessed to her teacher that she had committed all her geometry lessons to memory instead of reasoning them out. She could in this way satisfy a careless teacher who did not take the trouble to inquire how the pupil had prepared her lessons, but she knew little or no geometry.

The mind has what may be called three different levels. The first is the *sensory* level, represented by the phrase "in at one ear and out of the other." Every one has experienced reading a page when the mind would wander and only the eyes[9] follow the lines on down to the bottom of the page, nothing remaining as to the meaning of the text. It is easy to glance a lesson over just before reciting, and have it stick in the memory only long enough to serve the purposes of the recitation. Things learned in this way are not permanently serviceable and really constitute no part of an education.

The second level of the mind may be called the *memory* level. Matter which enters the mind only to this depth may be retained for a considerable time but is little understood and hence of small value. All rules and definitions committed without knowing their meaning or seeing their application, and all lessons learned merely to recite without a reasonable grasp of their meaning, sink only as deep as the memory level.

The third and deepest level is that of the *understanding*. Matter which permeates down through the sensory and memory levels, getting thoroughly into the understanding level, is not only remembered but is understood and applied, and therefore becomes of real service in our education. Of course it is clear that the ideal in teaching should be to[10] lead our pupils so to learn that most of what enters their memory shall also be mastered by their understanding.

Therefore, in the recitation we should test not alone to see what the pupil knows, but also to see *how he knows it*; not only to find out whether he can recite, but also what are his methods of learning. We should discover not alone whether the facts learned have entered the memory, but whether they have sunk down into the understanding, so that they can be used in the acquisition of further education.

c. The pupil's points of failure and the cause thereof. — Every teacher has been surprised many times to discover weak places in the pupil's work when everything had seemingly been thoroughly learned. With the best teaching these weak places will occasionally occur. It is not less essential to know these points of failure than to know the foundations of knowledge which the pupil has already mastered. For these weak spots must be remedied as we go along if the later work is to be successful. Very frequently classes are unable to proceed satisfactorily because of lack[11] of thoroughness in the foundation work which precedes. To know where a pupil is failing is the first requisite if we are to help him remedy his weakness.

But not only must the teacher know where the pupil is failing, but also the cause of his failure. Only when we know this can we intelligently apply the remedy for the failure. A physician friend of mine tells me that almost any quack can prescribe successfully for sickness if he has an expert at hand to diagnose the case and tell him what is the matter. This is the hardest part of a physician's work and requires the most skill. So it is with the teacher's work as well. If we are sure that a certain boy is failing in his recitations because he is lazy, it is not so difficult to devise a remedy to fit the case. If we know that another is failing because the work is too advanced for his preparation, we select a different remedy. But in every case we must first know the cause of failure if we hope to prescribe a remedy certain to produce a cure.

Some teachers prescribe for poorly learned lessons much after the patent medicine method.[12] A recent advertisement of one particular nostrum promises the cure of any one of thirty-seven different diseases. Surely with such a remedy as this at hand there will be no need to diagnose a case of sickness to find out what is the trouble. All we need to do is to take the regulation dose. And all patients will be treated just alike whatever their ailment. This is the quack doctor's method as it is the quack teacher's. If the teacher is unskillful or lazy the remedy for poor recitations usually is, "Take the same lesson for to-morrow." There is even no attempt to discover the cause of failure and no thought put on the question of how best to remedy the failure and prevent its recurrence.

4. *Teaching as an aim in the recitation*

While testing deals with the old,—reviewing and fixing more firmly that which we have already learned,—teaching, by using the old, leads on to the new. To *educate* means to *lead out*—to lead the child out from what he already has attained and mastered to new attainments and new mastery. This is accomplished through[13] teaching. It is not enough, therefore, to employ the recitation as a time for testing the class; the recitation is also the teacher's opportunity to teach. Teaching as distinguished from testing becomes, therefore, one of the great aims of the recitation.

Teaching should accomplish the following objects in the recitation:—

a. Give the child an opportunity for self-expression.—"We learn to do by doing," providing the doing is really ours. If the doing holds our interest and thought nothing will serve to clear up faulty thinking and partly mastered knowledge like attempting to express it. One really never fully knows a thing until he can so express it that others are caused to know it also.

Further, every person needs to cultivate the power of expression for its own sake. Expression consists not only of language, but the work of the hand in the various arts and handicrafts, bodily poise and carriage, facial expression, gesture, laughter, and any other means which the mind has of making itself known to others.[14] These various forms of expression are the only way we have of causing others to know what we think or feel. And the world cares very little how much we may know or how deeply we may feel if we have not the power to express our thoughts and emotions.

The child should have, therefore, the fullest possible opportunity in the recitation for as many of these different kinds of expression as are suitable to the work of the recitation. Not only must the teacher be careful not to monopolize the time of the class himself, but he must even lead the children out, encouraging them to express in their own words or through their drawings and pictures, or through maps they make or through the things they construct with their hands, or in any other way possible, their own knowledge and thought. The timid child who shrinks from reciting or going to the blackboard to draw or write needs encouragement and teaching especially. The constant danger with all teachers is that of calling upon the unusually quick and bright pupil who is ready to recite, thus giving him more than his share of training[15] in expression and robbing thereby the more timid ones who need the practice.

b. Give help on difficult points. — A complaint frequently heard in some schools, and no doubt in some degree merited in all, is, "Teacher will not help," or, "Teacher does not explain." No matter how excellent the work being done by the class or how skillful the teaching, there will always be hard points in the lessons which need analysis or explanation. This should usually be done when the lesson is assigned. A teacher who knows both the subject-matter and the class thoroughly can estimate almost precisely where the class will have trouble with the lesson, or what important points will need especial emphasis. And in the explanation and elaboration of these points is one of the best opportunities for good teaching. The good teacher will help just enough, but not too much; just enough so that the class will know how to go to work with the least loss of time and the greatest amount of energy; not enough so that the lesson is already mastered for the class before they begin their study.[16]

But it is necessary to help the class on the hard points not only in assigning the lesson, but also in the recitation. The alert teacher will in almost every recitation discover some points which the class have failed to understand or master fully. It is the overlooking of such half-mastered points as these that leaves weak places in the pupil's knowledge and brings trouble to him later on. These weak points left unstrengthened in the recitation are the lazy teacher's greatest reproach; the occasion of the unskillful teacher's greatest bungling; and the inexperienced teacher's greatest "danger points."

c. Bring in new points supplementing the text.—While the lesson of the textbook should be followed in the main, and most of the time devoted thereto, yet nearly every lesson gives the wide-awake teacher opportunity to supplement the text with interesting material drawn from other sources. This rightly done lends life and interest to the recitation, broadens the child's knowledge, and increases his respect for the teacher. In this way many lessons in history, geography, literature—in fact, in nearly all the[17] studies,—can have their application shown, and hence be made more real to the pupils.

d. Inspire the pupils to better efforts and higher ideals.—The recitation is the teacher's mental "point of contact" with his pupils. He meets them socially in a friendly way at intermissions and on the playground. His moral character and personality are a model to the children at all times. But it is chiefly in the recitation that the *mental* stimulus is given. The teacher who is lifeless and uninspiring in the teaching of the recitation cannot but fail to inspire his school to a strong mental growth, whatever else he may accomplish.

Most pupils have powers far in excess of those they are using. They only need to be inspired, to be wakened up mentally by a teacher whose mind is alive and growing. They need to be made hungry for education, and this can be accomplished only by a teacher who is himself full of enthusiasm. Inspiration is caught, not taught.

e. Lead pupils into good habits of study. — It is probably not too much to say that one third or one half of the pupil's time is lost in school be[18]cause of not knowing how to study. Over and over pupils say to the teacher, "I didn't know how to get this." Many times children labor hard over a lesson without mastering it, simply because they do not know how to pick out and classify its principal points. They work on what is to them a mere jumble, because they lack the power of analysis or have never been taught its use.

Very early in school life the pupil should be taught to look for and make a list of the principal points in the lesson. If the lesson starts with a Roman numeral I, the child should be taught to look for II and III, and to see how they are related to I. An Arabic 1 usually means that 2, and perhaps 3 and 4 are to follow; the letter *a* at the head of a paragraph should start the pupil to looking for *b, c,* etc. And if the text does not contain such numbering or lettering, the pupil should be led to search for the main divisions and topics of the lesson for himself.

Of course these principles will not apply to spelling lessons, mere lists of sentences to be analyzed or problems to be solved, but they do apply to almost every other type of lesson. The[19] best time to teach the child to make the kind of analysis suggested is when we are assigning the lesson. We can then go over the text with the class, helping them to select the chief points of the lesson until they themselves have learned this method of study.

5. *Drill as an aim in the recitation*

There is a great difference between merely knowing a thing and knowing it so well that we can use it easily and with skill. Perhaps all of us know the alphabet backwards; yet if the order of the dictionary were reversed so that it would run from Z to A, we would for a time lack the skill we now have in quickly finding any desired words in the dictionary.

Certain fundamentals in our education need to be so well learned that they are practically automatic, and can hence be skillfully performed without thought or attention. We must know our spelling in this way, so that we do not have to stop and think how to spell each word. In the same manner we must know the mechanics of reading, that is, the recognition and pronunci[20]ation of words, the meaning of punctuation marks, etc.; and similarly multiplication and the other fundamental operations in arithmetic. Pupils should come to know these things so well that they are as automatic as speech, or as walking, eating, or any other of the many acts which "do themselves." If this degree of skill is not reached, it means halting and inefficient work in all these lines farther on. Many are the children who are crippled in their work in history, geography, and other studies because they cannot read well enough to understand the text. Many are struggling along in the more advanced parts of the arithmetic, unable to master it because they are deficient in the fundamentals, because they lack skill. And many are wasting time trying to analyze sentences when they cannot recognize the different parts of speech.

Skill is efficiency in doing. It is always a growth, and never comes to us ready-made. To be sure, some pupils can develop skill much faster than others, but the point is, that *skill has to be developed*. Skill is the result of repetition, or practice, that is, of *drill*.[21]

The following principles should guide in the use of drill in the recitation:

a. Drill should be employed wherever a high degree of skill is required. — This applies to what have been called the "tools of knowledge," or those things which are necessary in order to secure all other knowledge. Such are the "three R's," reading, (w)riting, and (a)rithmetic, to which we may add spelling. Without a good foundation in these, all other knowledge will be up-hill work, if not wholly impossible.

b. Drill must be upon correct models, and with alert interest and attention. — Mere repetition is not enough to secure skill. What teacher has not been driven to her wits' ends to prevent the successive lines in the copy book from growing steadily worse as they increase in number from the copy on down the page! Surely drill with such a result would be long in arriving at skill. Such practice is not only wholly wasted, but actually results in establishing false models and careless habits in the pupil's mind. Each line must be written with correct models in mind, and with the effort to make it better[22] than any preceding one, if skill is to be the outcome.

Much of the value of drill is often lost through lack of interest and attention. The child lazily sing-songing the multiplication table may learn to say it as he would a verse of poetry, and yet not know the separate combinations when he needs them in problems. What he needs is drill upon the different combinations hit-and-miss, and in simple problems, rapidly and many times over, with sufficient variety and spice, so that his interest and attention are always alert. A certain boy persisted in saying "have went" instead of "have gone." Finally his teacher said, "Johnny, you may stay to-night after school and write 'have gone' on the blackboard one hundred times. Then you will not miss it again."

Johnny stayed after school and wrote "have gone" one hundred times as the teacher had directed. When he had completed his task the teacher had gone to another part of the building. Before leaving for home Johnny politely left this note on the teacher's desk: "Dear Teacher: I have went home." Plenty of drill, but it was not[23] accompanied by interest and attention, and hence left no effect.

c. Drill must not stop short of a reasonable degree of efficiency, or skill.—Most teachers would rather *test* or *teach* than *drill*. Others do not see the necessity of drill. Hence it happens that a large proportion of our pupils are not given practice or drill enough to arrive at even a fair degree of skill. Set ten pupils of the intermediate grades to adding up four columns of figures averaging a footing of 100 to the column, and you will probably have at least five different answers. And so with many of the fundamentals in other branches as well. *We too often stop practice just short of efficiency, and thereby waste both time and effort.*

d. Drill must be governed by definite aims.—Probably drilling requires more planning and care on the part of the teacher than any other work of the recitation. Drill applied indiscriminately wastes time and kills interest. To study a spelling lesson over fifteen times as some teachers require is folly. Every spelling list will contain some words which the pupil already knows. He[24] should put little or no drill on these, but only on the troublesome ones. In learning and using the principal parts of verbs it is always the few that cause the difficulty. "He *done* it"; "Has the bell *rang*?" "*Set* down." These and a few other forms are the ones which give the trouble; they should receive the drill. Likewise in arithmetic, there are certain combinations in the tables, and certain operations in fractions, measurements, etc., which always make trouble. They are the "danger points," and upon these the practice should be put.

The teacher must aim, therefore, to select the difficult and the important points and drill upon these until they are mastered, being careful not to stop at the "half-way house," but steadily to go on until skill is obtained. He must be resourceful in methods and devices which will relieve the monotony of repetition; he must be persistent and patient, insisting on the attainment of skill, but realizing that it takes time to develop it; he must possess a good pedagogical conscience which will be satisfied with nothing short of success in his aims.[25]

6. *A desirable balance among the three aims*

The aims to be accomplished through the recitation are, then, *testing, teaching*, and *drilling*. These three aims may, as said before, all be carried on in the same recitation, or they may come in different recitations, as the needs of the subject require. Not infrequently they may alternate with each other within a few moments. In every case, however, the teacher should have clearly in mind which one of the three processes he is employing and why. Not that the teacher must always stop to reason the matter out before he employs one or the other, but that he should become so familiar with the nature and use of each that he almost unconsciously passes from one to the other as the need for it arises.

Not many teachers are equally skilled in the use of testing, teaching, and drilling. Some have a tendency to put most of the recitation time on testing whether the class have prepared the assignment, and devote but little time to teaching or drilling. Others love to teach, but do not like to test or drill. It is highly desirable that every[26] teacher, young or old in experience, should examine himself on this question and, if he finds himself lacking in any one of the three, carefully set to work to remedy the defect. The ideal for us all to reach is equal skill in each of the three processes of the recitation, testing, teaching, and drilling.

[29]

II

THE METHOD OF THE RECITATION

1. *Method varies with aim*

In the last chapter we discussed the aims or purposes of the recitation. We now come to see how these aims affect the methods we employ. For it is evident at the outset that the method we choose must depend on the aim sought in the recitation. If we seek to-day to make the recitation chiefly a test of how well the lesson has been prepared, or how much of yesterday's work has been retained, we will select a method suited for *testing*. If we aim to introduce the class to the subject of percentage for the first time, the method must be adapted to *teaching*. If we wish to make the recitation a drill in the diacritical markings or the multiplication table, the method must be still a different one. In other words, *the method must be planned to accomplish certain[30] definite ends if the teaching is to be purposeful and effective.*

2. *Fundamental principles of method*

There are certain fundamental principles of method which underlie all teaching, and which, therefore, are to be sought in every recitation, no matter what the special method used may chance to be. The first of these principles may be stated as follows: —

a. Interest is the first requisite for attention and all mental activity. — A recitation without interest is a dead recitation. Because it possesses no life it cannot lead to growth. Nothing can take the place of interest. Fear may drive to work for a time, but it does not result in development. Only interest can bring all the powers and capacities of the child into play. Hence the teacher's first and greatest problem in the recitation is the problem of interest. To secure interest he must use every resource at his command. This does not mean that he is to bid for the children's interest with sensational methods and cheap devices. This is not the way to secure[31] true interest. It means, rather, that he is to offer to the class subject-matter suited to their age and experience, and presented in a way adapted to their capacity and understanding; that he is to have all conditions surrounding the recitation as favorable as possible; and that he is himself to be constantly a source of interest and enthusiasm. If these conditions are all met the problem of interest will present few difficulties.

b. The natural mode of learning is to proceed from the known to the related unknown.—This is a statement of what is known as the principle of *apperception* or the learning of the new by connecting it with the old already in the mind. To make use of this principle it is necessary to freshen up what the pupil knows on a topic by asking him questions or otherwise causing him to think anew the facts previously learned that are related to what he is about to learn. For example, when beginning the subject of percentage, the subject of decimals should be reviewed, since percentage is but an application of decimals and can most easily be learned and understood[32] as such. Likewise in beginning the study of the Civil War, the question of slavery and that of the doctrine of states' rights should be reviewed, since these are fundamental to an understanding of the causes of the war. In similar manner we might apply the illustration to every branch of study, Indeed there is hardly a single recitation which should not start with a brief review or a few questions to freshen up in the minds of the pupils the points related to the coming lesson. Not only will this insure that the lessons themselves shall be better understood, but the entire subject will in this way come to possess a unity instead of consisting of a series of more or less disconnected lessons in the mind of the child.

3. *The use of special forms of method*

Having stated these two general principles of method, we will now consider some of the special forms of method to be employed in the recitation. In discussing these methods and comparing them it is not to be forgotten that attention and interest are dependent in large measure on change and variety. The same method used day after[33] day in the recitation palls upon a class and invites listlessness and inattention. A teacher should never employ cheap or sensational devices in a recitation just to have something new, but neither should he work a good method to death by too constant use.

4. *The question-and-answer method*

The question-and-answer method is so familiar to every one that it requires no formal definition. It is employed in all grades from the primary to the university, and it is adapted alike to testing, teaching, and drilling.

This method admits of wide modification to suit it to specific uses. The questions asked may require but a short and simple answer, such as can be given by a primary pupil. They may also require a long and complex answer which will test the powers of the most advanced student. The questions may be detailed and searching, covering every point of the lesson, as when we are testing preparation. They may deal only with certain related truths, as when we "develop" a new subject intentionally by questions and an[34]swers. Or they may select only the most important points upon which the class needs drill.

a. When and where to employ the question-and-answer method. — The question-and-answer method is particularly adapted to the lower grades, in which the children have not yet developed the ability to recite independently on long topics. This method allows the teacher to encourage and draw out the child by what is really a conversation between the two, the teacher asking simple questions and the child responding to them. In more advanced grades the questions may be so arranged as to require longer and more complex answers, and thus lead up to the topical method of reciting.

The question-and-answer method is also suitable to employ at the beginning of a recitation to recall to the minds of the class previous lessons to which the lesson of the day is related. There is hardly one recitation in a hundred that does not require an introduction of this kind. The only true method in teaching is to build the new knowledge on the related old knowledge which is already in the mind. This is what is meant in[35] pedagogy by "proceeding from the known to the related unknown." And the known must always be fresh and immediately present to the mind. Hence the necessity for the introductory review.

This method is also serviceable in reviewing former lessons. By the use of well-selected questions a large number of important points already passed over can be brought before the class in a short time.

On the whole, it is probable that we do not review frequently enough in our recitation work. We review a subject when we have finished the text upon it, or before examination time, but this is not enough. Careful psychological tests have shown that the mind forgets within the first three days a large proportion of what it will finally fail to retain. Further, there is great economy in catching up a fading fact before it gets wholly away from us. This would suggest the constant use of the question-and-answer method to fix more firmly the important points in ground we have already passed over.

One of the most important uses of this method[36] is found in *inductive teaching*. The famous "Socratic method" was simply the question-and-answer method applied by Socrates to teaching new truths. This noted teacher would, by a series of skillful questions calculated to call forth what the pupil already knew, lead him on to new knowledge without actually telling the youth anything himself. And this is the very height of good teaching — the goal toward which we all should strive.

It is a safe maxim never to tell a child what one can lead him by questioning to see for himself. To illustrate: Suppose an elementary arithmetic class already know thoroughly how to find the area of a rectangle by multiplying its base by its altitude, and that we are now ready to teach them how to find the area of a triangle. Let us see whether we can lead them to "develop" the rule instead of learning it out of the text; that is, we will proceed inductively. First draw a rectangle 4 by 6 on the board.

Q. What do we call this figure?

A. A rectangle.

Q. How shall we find its area?[37]

A. Multiply its base 4 by its altitude 6; the area is 24.

Q. Now I draw a line diagonally across the rectangle; how many figures are there?

A. Two. (Teacher here gives new word "triangle" and explains it.)

Q. How do the base and altitude of the triangles compare with the base and altitude of the rectangle?

A. They are the same.

Q. How do the two triangles compare in area?

A. They are equal; each is half of the rectangle.

Q. Then, if each is half of the rectangle, what must be the area of one of the triangles?

A. The area of each triangle is 12, for the area of the rectangle is 24, and the area of each triangle is half that of the rectangle.

Q. Then, how may we find the area of a triangle?

A. Multiply the base by the altitude and take one half the product.

Of course the teacher may have to supplement questions like the above by others to assist[38] the child in arriving at the desired answer, but the method is the same in any case. The inductive method is the child's natural way of learning, and should be applied to nearly all school branches. Too many teachers have children learn rules and definitions which mean little or nothing to them. This is not only discouraging to the child and a serious waste of time, but it develops bad habits of study by making the pupil think he is learning something when he is not. Only when the fact or process learned is *understood* is it true knowledge. The inductive method begins with what the child already knows and, step by step, leads him to understand the new truths. It comes last to the rule or definition after the meaning is clearly seen.

b. Dangers of the question-and-answer method. — No matter how good a method may be, there are always some dangers connected with its use, some points at which a teacher needs to be on guard to see that the method is not misused or over-used. The question-and-answer method is no exception to this rule.

One of the greatest dangers in the use of this[39] method is that pupils will come to depend on the questions as a crutch to help them along mentally when they should be able to proceed by themselves. Not infrequently do pupils say to the teacher when called upon for a topical discussion, "If you will ask me questions upon the topic I can answer them, but I cannot recite upon the topic." It is very much easier to answer a series of questions upon a subject than to discuss it independently. This method is well adapted to younger children; and this very reason makes it a danger when over-used with more advanced pupils. We need to learn to think a subject through and talk about topics without the help of a teacher to stand by and ask questions; we need to become independent in our thinking; we need practice in organizing and expressing our thoughts for ourselves.

The second danger we note in the question-and-answer method is that it does not give as much opportunity for training in self-expression as the topical method. In teaching by the question-and-answer method, the teacher occupies nearly or quite as much time with the questions as the class do[40] with the answers. This does not give opportunity for practice enough in reciting on the part of the pupil, if the question-and-answer method is employed exclusively. The only way for a child to learn to recite well is by reciting; the only way to learn to express one's self is by having opportunity for expression.

5. *The topical method*

The topical method is too familiar to require definition. In this method the teacher suggests a topic of the lesson or asks a question which requires the pupil to go on in his own way and tell what he can about the point under discussion. There is really no hard and fast line between the topical method and the question-and-answer method. The fundamental difference between the two is this: In the question-and-answer method, the question is definitely upon some fact or point, and requires a specific answer bearing on the fact or point of the question; in the topical method, the question or topic suggested requires the pupil to decide upon what facts or points need discussion, and then to plan his own discussion.[41]

a. Where the topical method is most serviceable. — As has already been explained, the topical method requires more independence of thought than the question-and-answer method, and will therefore find its greatest use in the higher grades. We are not to think, however, that the topical method is not to be used until some certain grade has been reached, and that then the child will suddenly find himself able to use it. The ability to think independently and speak one's thoughts freely is a growth, and is not attained suddenly at a given age. Even little children, telling their language stories, are using the topical method, and should be encouraged in its use. As the grades advance, however, the use of this method should increase, and the length and difficulty of the topics should grow, so that recitation by topics can be efficiently carried on in the higher intermediate and grammar grades.

Probably the easiest forms of the topical recitation are found in history or reading lessons, where *narration* abounds. Narration deals with a succession of events, and is always found one of the easiest forms of discourse. In proof of this, one[42] has but to note the fluency and ease with which a child will narrate the events of a game, a trip, or an accident, whereas if you call upon him for logical explanations or even for description, as for example, "Just what kind of looking team was it that ran away?" much more difficulty will be experienced in telling about it.

Another great field for topical recitations is found in all lines where *description* is required. This applies to all nature study and science, to geography, to certain phases of literature and history. To describe even a commonplace object accurately and well is an art more rare than most of us would think. Suppose you ask the first person you meet to describe fully the house in which he lives or the sunset which he has just seen. If he seriously tries to comply with your request, you will probably be surprised both by the difficulty he has in his attempt, and the little that he really can say upon these familiar subjects. The interesting story teller is a rarity, which is only another way of saying that the ability to narrate and describe needs cultivation. There is no better opportunity possible than that of the topical recitation.[43]

The topical method can manifestly be used to supplement the question-and-answer method in testing the pupils on the preparation of the lesson, or in reviewing former lessons. It can also be well used in teaching new subject-matter which does not particularly require the developmental, or "Socratic," method. Illustrations of such material are to be found in much of the work in history and in literature; also in the descriptive parts of geography, nature study, and science.

When the topical method is being employed it will nearly always need to be supplemented by questions and answers. Very rarely will a pupil recite upon any important topic with such accuracy and completeness that nothing more needs to be said concerning it. Hence, after the pupil has completed his topical discussion, the teacher can round out the subject, impress the more important points, or correct wrong impressions, by a few questions to be answered either by the pupil who has had the discussion or by the remainder of the class.

The topical method gives the teacher the best opportunity to teach the pupils how to study. It[44] is safe to say that most pupils consider that they "have their lesson" when they understand it, or think they can remember it. But if the child is to be taught expression, as well as given knowledge, it is evident that this is not enough. Not only should a pupil be sure that he understands his lesson and can remember it, but also he should think how best to express it in the recitation. The teacher can help the class in this when assigning the topics by showing the pupils how to pick out the main points of the topics, and arrange them in order for discussion. This is, of course, really training in analysis—a power that all pupils need to cultivate.

b. The question of standards in topical recitations.—The success of the topical method will depend much on the teacher's standards of thoroughness applied to its use. Children, particularly of the lower grades, have not yet developed much grasp of mind, and consequently are not able to judge when they have sufficiently covered a topic given them for recitation. They are likely to think that if they stand up and say *something* about the topic, this is sufficient.[45]

It is at this point that the teacher needs to exercise great care. The child must not be discouraged by harsh criticism, but neither must an incomplete recitation be accepted as a complete one. The teacher must judge carefully how full a discussion should be expected from a child of the given age, taking into account the treatment of the topic in the pupil's textbook. Then by questions, further discussion by other pupils, kindly criticisms, and helpful suggestions, the standard should be placed as high as the class can attain. Nor is it to be forgotten that the standard is to be a constantly advancing one.

6. The lecture, or supplemental method

The lecture method is rather too formal a name for the method in which the teacher talks to the class instead of asking them to recite. He may either take the entire period in a lecture, or talk, or he may only supplement now and then the answers or topical recitations of the pupils. This method is almost exclusively used in many universities and colleges, but is not suited for extensive use in more elementary schools.[46]

a. How the lecture method is to be used.—While the lecture method should be employed sparingly in the elementary school, yet it is most valuable to supplement other methods. First, in introducing a class to a new subject or section of work, it is frequently desirable that the teacher should take a part or the whole of a recitation period to explain the nature of the work or to interest the pupils in it. For example: In taking up the discovery of America, the teacher can create interest by telling the class of the wonderful events going on in Europe during the fifteenth century, of the life of Columbus as a boy, of the ships then in use, comparing them with our present steamships, etc. Similarly for almost every new section taken up in any study.

The lecture method is also useful in supplementing the recitations of the pupils. The teacher's knowledge must be much broader than the textbook; and a little explanation added, an incident told, or an application of the lesson made will often do much to broaden the pupil's knowledge of the subject, and will at the same[47] time lend interest to the recitation, besides increasing respect for the teacher's education. There is nothing more deadening to the recitation than a mechanical plodding through the questions and answers of a textbook without any explanation or amplification, and often without much comprehension on the part of the class. The teacher who has nothing of his own to add is incapable of *teaching* in the true sense of the word. At best he can only *test* as to the preparation from the textbook.

b. Dangers from the lecture method.—While we justly condemn the teacher who has nothing of his own to add to the recitation, we must not forget that there is a danger on the other side. Ask any assemblage of teachers how many think that, in general, their own teachers used to talk too much in the recitation, thereby monopolizing the time, and two thirds will blame their former teachers for over-using the lecture method. Most people, when they are sure of an audience, like to talk, and probably teachers are no exception to the rule.

The teacher who is full of information and[48] enthusiasm for the recitation is led by this very fact into temptation. Some point in the lesson suggests an interesting story or illustration, or some additional bit of information, and the teacher starts to tell it to the class. He becomes himself so interested in it that the lesson is forgotten and the class period ended long before the story is completed. This may do occasionally; but, once it becomes a habit, it is fatal to good teaching. The recitation as prepared by the class should be the chief interest of the class period. The teacher must learn to supplement without monopolizing.

7. The written recitation

The written recitation can hardly be called a method, since it can be itself applied to any or all of the methods of reciting. Like all other methods, the written recitation has its strong points of excellence and also its dangers.

a. The use of the written recitation. — The written recitation is especially useful in cases where all of the class should recite upon all of the lesson. It is easy to see that by having each of a class of ten answer ten questions, a far larger amount[49] of answering is done in the aggregate than if only one could answer at a time, as in oral recitation.

There are certain kinds of knowledge that are seldom used except in writing. For example, we are never called upon to spell or to use letter forms, business forms, punctuation marks, etc., except in writing. It is safe to say that matter of such kinds should usually be taught by having it written.

The written recitation also leads to accuracy and precision of thought and expression. We all formulate more carefully what we write than what we speak.

The written recitation also gives an opportunity for training in verbal expression. Every person needs to be able to express himself easily and forcibly in writing. But this requires much practice, and there is no better practice than in formulating in writing the thoughts of the daily lessons.

b. Dangers in the use of the written method. — Valuable as the written method is, there are certain cautions to be observed in its use.

This method does not ordinarily possess the interest and spontaneity of the oral recitation.[50] There is no opportunity for the teacher to supplement with points brought in. Misconceptions are not cleared up in the minds of the pupils, at least during that recitation period, unless the written papers are read at once. Usually time does not permit this. Many children do not like to write, and hence find the lesson tiresome, especially if continued for a whole class period.

The amount of writing required of children may be too great. Few pupils can write long at a time without eye-strain, muscle cramp, and bad bodily positions. Where this is the case, over-fatigue results if the amount of written work required is large. It is not unusual to find schools in which children are required to spend almost half of their school hours in some form of written work. This is a serious mistake both educationally and from the standpoint of health.

There is also still another side of the matter to consider. One of the great advantages of written work is that the pupil may have his errors shown him, so that he may reflect upon them and correct them. But not infrequently, where the amount of written work is too large, the er[51]rors are not carefully corrected by the teacher, and not corrected at all by the pupil. This is why many pupils will keep on making the same error time after time on their papers. The correction has not sufficiently impressed them.

All written work, with perhaps rare exceptions, should be carefully gone over by the teacher, and all serious or oft-repeated errors corrected by the pupils who make them. Not infrequently may children be seen to glance over a paper upon which the teacher has put precious time and some red ink in making corrections, and then crumple the paper and throw it into the waste basket. Sometimes this is done in sheer carelessness, and sometimes in petulance because of the many corrections. This is all a loss of time and opportunity. The teacher should have tact enough to show the pupils that corrections are made on their papers for their benefit, and not as a punishment. And then the pupils should take the trouble to correct the errors, that they may not occur again. Better a thousand times correct carefully an old paper than write a new one containing the same errors.

[55]

III

THE ART OF QUESTIONING

1. *The importance of good questioning*

Skill in the art of questioning lies at the basis of all good teaching. When we were children it looked so easy for the teacher to sit and ask the questions which we were expected to answer. When we become teachers we find that it is much harder to ask the questions than to answer them. For to question well, one must not only know the subject thoroughly, but must also constantly interpret the mind of the pupil to discover what question next to ask, and whether he is mastering what we are teaching him.

Good questioning stimulates thought, leads to inquiry, and results in understanding and mastery. Poor questioning leaves the mental powers unawakened, cripples thought, and results in inefficiency and lack of mastery.[56]

2. *Need of fundamental principles*

Good questioning is dependent upon the teacher's having a firm command of a few essential principles which apply to all questioning used in teaching. The teacher's constant self-criticism in the light of these will greatly improve his control of discussion in the class room.

3. *The principle of freedom from textbooks*

The questions of the recitation must of course deal with the matter of the textbook and be directly suggested by it. Yet there are two dangers to be avoided in this connection: (1) Questions should not follow the language of the text, and (2) the teacher should not be dependent on the textbook to suggest the question itself or to determine the correctness of the answer.

The teacher who has not the lesson well prepared, or who is mentally lazy, has a constant temptation to ask questions in the words of the book. This is much easier than to know the subject and the text-book both well enough to formulate original, appropriate questions. An[57] illustration of what is meant is found in the following account of a recitation conducted from "Montgomery's American History," the lesson being on the landing of the Pilgrims (pp. 77, 78): —

Q. On a morning late in November, what did the Pilgrims do?

A. They sighted Cape Cod.

Q. Two days later, where did the Mayflower come to anchor?

A. In Provincetown Harbor.

Q. While the Mayflower remained at anchor, what did Captain Standish and a boatload of men do?

A. They went out to explore.

Q. On the shore of Plymouth harbor what is there lying?

A. A granite bowlder.

It is seen that each of these questions follows the words of the text, and that the answer but completes the sentence of which the question is a part. Questions of this kind only suggest to the memory the statement of the text, and do not cause the pupil to use his own thought in[58] realizing the actual event. Hence they arouse little interest and leave little impression. They train the verbal memory, but leave imagination, thought, and understanding untouched. How much better such questions as these: —

When did the Pilgrims first sight land?

What land did they see?

What was its appearance?

Have you ever seen a stretch of shore like this one?

Why did not the Pilgrims land at this point?

Where did they finally anchor?

What measures did they take to see whether this was a suitable place to land?

Why is the name "Plymouth Rock" so famous in American history?

These questions cover just the same ground as the ones above, but they suggest living pictures and actual events rather than the language of the textbook.

The unprepared or lazy teacher is also in danger of relying on the textbook for his questions even when he does not formulate them in the language of the printed page. Not infrequently[59] teachers conduct the whole of a recitation with the text open before them, hardly taking their eyes from the book, and seeming to have no inspiration or questions not immediately gleaned from the page before them. In extreme cases of unpreparedness they may even have to test the correctness of the answers given by the class by reference to the text. Of course this is all the highest degree of inefficiency. It should not be called teaching at all, for no one can teach another that which he does not himself possess as a part of his own mental equipment. Nothing can be more deadening to a class than to see a teacher, whom they look upon as their intellectual leader, floundering in such a vain attempt to teach something that he does not himself know.

The eyes and the mind of the teacher must both be free in the recitation — the eyes to look interest and encouragement into the eyes of the class, the mind to marshal the points of the lesson and watch the effects of their presentation on the minds of the pupils. A recitation at its best consists of an animated and interesting conversation between teacher and class. And no[60] conversation can be live and interesting when one of its participants has mind and eyes riveted to a book; for conversation involves an interchange of expression, of spirit, and of personality as well as of words.

It is not meant that a teacher must never have a textbook open before him during a recitation. Often it is not only desirable, but necessary that he should do so; but only for suggestion and reference, and never to supply questions and test answers.

It is certainly much better to have the textbook before one than to teach the lesson after a disconnected and haphazard fashion from lack of familiarity with its points. An excellent substitute for the text, however, is an outline, or plan of the lesson embodying the main points, illustrations, and applications to be made. Such an outline will save the teacher from wandering too far afield in the discussions, will insure unity in the lesson, and make certain that important points shall not be overlooked.

A desirable rule for the teacher to set for himself would be so to prepare for the recitation by[61] mastery of the subject, and by lesson plan or outline, *that he does not need to have the textbook open before him when the pupils do not also have their books open.* The teacher who will heroically meet this standard will soon find growing in himself a feeling of mastery of his subjects and of joy in his teaching.

4. *The principle of unity or continuity in questions*

Questions should be so planned that they develop or bring out the unity of the lesson. It is possible for questions to be so haphazard and disconnected that the pupil receives the impression of a series of unrelated facts, rather than a unified and related subject. In good questioning, one question naturally grows out of another, so that the series develops step by step the truth contained in the lesson, and brings it to the mind of the child as a complete whole.

This means that the teacher must know the whole subject so thoroughly that the right questions come to him easily and naturally, and in the right order to bring out the successive steps of the lesson in their logical relations.[62]

The difference between a related series of questions and an unrelated is shown in two lists which follow. Both deal with the same subject-matter, a physiology lesson on respiration. The questions of the first list are not themselves faulty, but there is no continuity among them; one does not grow out of another so as to "develop" the subject in the minds of the class.

What change takes place in the air while in the lungs?

What change takes place in the blood while in the lungs?

How many cubic inches of air will the lungs contain?

How much of this cannot be expelled by breathing out?

How many times do we naturally breathe in a minute?

What are some of the effects of breathing impure air?

How is the oxygen carried by the blood?

What is animal heat?

What is the temperature of the body?

These questions were all answered fairly well[63] by the class, but the answers contained only so many bits of isolated information, and the pupils did not understand the subject after they had recited upon it. Another teacher asked the following questions:

Why must the body have air to breathe?

Of what use is oxygen in the body?

Where does this oxidization, or burning up of worn-out cells, take place?

But how is the oxygen carried to every part of the body and brought into contact with the tissues?

Where do the corpuscles of the blood get their loads of oxygen?

What gas do they give up in exchange for the oxygen?

Where do they get the carbon dioxide?

How does air entering the lungs differ from air leaving them?

What corresponding change takes place in the blood while it is in the lungs?

Explain how the change is effected in each case.

Suppose we breathe air that contains too little oxygen, what will be the effect on the corpuscles?[64]

What will be the effect on oxidization in the tissues?

And what is the effect of poor oxidization on physical vitality?

On mental vitality?

The class that answered these questions not only had the information belonging to each separate question, but also understood the lesson as a whole, because each question grew out of the ones that preceded it, thus making the recitation a unified whole.

5. *The principle of clearness*

Questions must be made clear, so that their meaning may be understood. This is not always an easy task, and the teacher frequently misses being wholly clear. This is evidenced by the fact that often when a pupil fails to answer a question asked in one way, he can answer it easily when the wording is changed. This means that the difficulty for the pupil existed in the question, and not in the answer.

Clearness in questioning involves three factors: (1) Freedom from ambiguity or obscurity of word[65]ing; (2) adaptation to the age and understanding of the pupil; (3) reasonable brevity.

a. Freedom from ambiguity or obscurity of wording.—This is fundamentally a matter of the use of good English. It requires such a choice and arrangement of words and clauses that there can be no doubt as to the meaning to be conveyed. Assuming a fair command of the language and care in its use, the basis of clearness at this point is thorough mastery of the subject-matter of the questions, so that the teacher himself understands clearly just what he means to ask.

The following illustrations show some questions that are faulty from the standpoint of obscurity of meaning:—

What caused Lincoln to issue the Emancipation Proclamation in 1863? (Not clear whether question means why did he issue the Emancipation Proclamation at all, or why did he issue it in 1863 instead of at some other time.)

What are the effects of attention to a moving object? (Not clear whether question means effects on the person attending or the effect which the moving of an object has in making itself seen.)[66]

Who chased whom down what valley?

Why has a cat fur and a duck feathers?

b. Adaptation to the age and understanding of the child.—Questions that are perfectly clear to an adult may be hazy or incomprehensible to a child because he does not understand the terms used in the question, or because it deals with matters beyond his grasp. The teacher must keep within the vocabulary of the child in formulating his questions. Where it is necessary or desirable to introduce new words into questions, care must be taken that the child knows fully the meaning of the new terms. A teacher asked a class in elementary physiology, "What measures would you take to resuscitate a person asphyxiated with carbon dioxide?" The class all looked blank. No one seemed to know what to do. It chanced that the superintendent was visiting the school, and he said to the teacher, "Let me try." Then he asked the class, "What would you do for a person who had been smothered by breathing coal gas?" The class brightened up, and every hand was raised indicating readiness to answer the question.

Another teacher bewildered his class by asking,[67] "Which phenomena of the fratricidal strife in the American Republic were most determinative of the ultimate fate of the nation?" No one knew. Had he asked his question in plain terms, no doubt the class could have answered it.

In an elementary history class, a teacher propounded this question: "What American institutions have been founded on the principle of social democracy?" Not only the terms of the question, but the thought also is beyond the comprehension of children. Such questions are not only useless as a means of testing, teaching, or drilling, but serve to confuse and discourage the child, and cause him to lose interest in school.

c. Brevity.—No matter how well a question is worded, or how well it is adapted to the age and capacity of the pupil, it may fail in clearness because it is too long and disjointed, or because it deals with too many points. Far better break a complicated question up into several simple ones, concerning whose meaning there can be no doubt.

A teacher who had not yet mastered the art of questioning asked his physiology class a question somewhat like this: "Do you consider it advis[68]able, taking into account the fact that none of the vital processes go on as vigorously during sleep as during the waking hours (you remember that the breathing and the pulse are less rapid and the temperature of the body also lower), to eat just before retiring at night, especially if one is very tired and exhausted—a condition which still further lowers the vitality and hence decreases the powers of digestion and assimilation, and would your answer be different if it is understood that the food taken is to be light and easily digested?"

It is needless to say that the class found themselves lost in the maze of conditions and parenthetical expressions and did not attempt an answer. The question contains material for a dozen different questions, and probably the class could have answered them all had they been properly asked.

6. *The principle of definiteness*

Questions should be definite, so that they can have but one meaning. It is possible to ask a question so that its general meaning is clear enough, but so that its *precise* meaning is in doubt. Such questions leave the pupil puzzled,[69] and usually lead to indirectness or guessing in the answer. Failure to make questions definite, so that they can have but one meaning is responsible for much of the difference of opinion on disputed questions.

Many a stock question upon which amateur debating societies have exercised their talents would admit of no debate at all, if once the question were made definite. For the ground for debate lies in the difference in interpretation of the question and not in the facts themselves. For example: If a cannon ball were to be fired off by some mechanical device a million miles from where there was any ear to hear, would there be any sound? The lack of definiteness here which permits difference of opinion lies in the word "sound." If we add after the word "sound" the phrase, "in the sense of a conscious auditory sensation," the answer would obviously be, No, since there can be no auditory sensation without an ear to hear it. If, on the other hand, instead of the above phrase we add, "in the sense of wave-vibrations in the air," the answer will obviously be, Yes, since the wave-vibrations in the air do[70] not depend on the presence of an ear to be affected by them.

Likewise, in the question, If a man starts to walk around a squirrel which is clinging to the limb of a tree, and if, as the man circles the tree, the squirrel also circles the tree so that he constantly faces the man, when the man has gone completely around the tree, has he gone around the squirrel? Here the indefiniteness lies in the meaning of to "go around." With this indefiniteness remedied, there is no longer any possibility of difference of opinion.

Indefiniteness may come from the use of certain words that from their very nature are indefinite in meaning. Such are the verbs *be*, *do*, *have*, *become*, *happen*, and the prepositions *of* and *about*. Examples of indefiniteness growing out of such colorless words are found in the following questions, which are types of many asked in our schools daily: —

What does water *do* when heated? (Expands, evaporates, boils.)

What *happens* when it lightnings? (Thunder, discharge of electricity, flash.)[71]

What must immigrants coming into this country *have*? (Money, freedom from disease, character.)

What did Arnold *become*? (A traitor, a British general, an outcast, a repentant man.)

What *is* the cow? (A mammal, a quadruped, a producer of milk, butter, and beef; an herbivorous animal.)

What *about* the Monroe Doctrine? (A dozen different things.)

What *of* the animals in the temperate zone?

Questions may be so general as to be indefinite. The teacher asks, "Where is Chicago?" The class may answer, "In Illinois on Lake Michigan; in North America; in Cook County." The teacher should know just what answer he desires, and then ask, "In what State; on what continent; on what lake; or in what county?"

Other illustrations of vagueness coming from the use of words of too general a meaning are found in such questions as, What *kind* of man was George Washington?

When does a person need food?

How does tobacco grow?[72]

What do birds like?

All indefinite questions deserve and usually receive an indefinite answer, and hence lead to and encourage guessing. If the answers to such questions as the above are not indefinite, they must be purely memoriter, merely reproducing the words of the text without comprehension of any real meaning.

Indefinite questioning usually comes from a lack of clear thinking on the part of the questioner. The teacher himself does not know precisely what he means to ask, and hence cannot be definite. It is safe to say that the teacher's questions covering a subject will never be any more clear or definite than the subject itself is in his mind. Indeed it is hard for one to be wholly definite in questioning even when he is a perfect master of his subject. Certainly, then, eternal vigilance will be the price of clearness and definiteness on the part of the young teacher who is as yet striving for mastery of what he is teaching.[73]

7. Secondary principles of good questioning

Besides the foregoing fundamental principles underlying the art of questioning, there are a few secondary principles, some of which are of hardly less importance: —

1. Questions should be asked naturally, and in a conversational tone, and not explosively *demanded* of pupils.

2. Usually the question should be addressed to the entire class and, after all have had a moment to think, some one then designated to answer. The reason for this is obvious. If the one who is to answer is designated before the question is asked, the incentive to the rest of the class to think the answer is greatly lessened.

3. No regular order should be followed in calling on pupils. If such an order is established, the lazy and uninterested ones have a tendency to remain inactive until called upon. By the hit-and-miss method of calling no one knows at what moment he may be the next one, hence there is a strong incentive to attend to the lesson. It is also desirable to call on a pupil occasionally the[74] second time very soon after he has previously been called upon. This prevents him from thinking that as soon as he has recited once he can then safely relax his attention.

4. Inattentive or mischievous pupils should be the mark for frequent questions. If it comes to be known that any inattention is sure to bring questions to the pupil at fault, the battle for attention is half won. There is a strong tendency on the part of the teacher to ask for the answer to a question from those whose eyes show that they are attentive and ready with an answer. While this readiness and atten-

tion should be rewarded by giving an opportunity to answer, it must not lead the teacher to neglect those who may need the question more than the more ready ones. The questions should be impartially distributed among the bright and the dull pupils.

5. It is highly important that questions shall be asked so that they demand thought in answering, and usually so that the answer must be given in a full statement. Seldom should a question be asked in such form that a simple Yes or No will answer it. This does not require sufficient[75] thought on the part of the pupil, it permits guess-work, and fails to cultivate ability in expression. Answers that may be given in a word or two, or by Yes or No, may be accepted in rapid drill or review work, and also in the inductive questioning used in developing a new subject, but should be used very sparingly in other places in the recitation.

6. The "pumping" question should not be used. In this type of question, the teacher formulates the answer and leaves only the key word for the pupil to supply. The teacher sometimes goes so far as to suggest the necessary word by pronouncing the first syllable or two of it. A dialogue like the following was heard in one school: —

Q. "Columbus was an − −?"

A. "Explorer."

Q. "No, he was an It − −?"

A. "Oh, an Italian."

Such an attempt at teaching would be amusing, were it not so serious for the child.[76]

8. The treatment of answers

The teacher's treatment of the answers given is of hardly less importance than the formulation of the questions themselves. It is to be remembered that the recitation is an interchange of thought and expression between teacher and class. To this end, the response must be mutual. Not alone when the question is being asked is the teacher to be animated and interested, but likewise while the answer is being given. It is neither good pedagogy nor good manners for a teacher to sit unresponsive and inattentive when a pupil is reciting. Not that the teacher needs always to comment on an answer, or say that it is correct; it is rather a matter of manner, of attention and interest to the answer. We find it embarrassing either in a recitation or out of it to talk to a person who seems not to be listening.

Right at this point, however, there lurks an insidious danger. It comes easily and naturally to one to give some sign of assent or disapproval as to the correctness of the answer while it is[77] being spoken. The slightest inclination of the head, the dropping of the eyelids, or a certain expression of the face, comes to be read by the pupil as a signboard to guide him in his statements. This is, of course, all wrong. The teacher should give absolutely no sign while the answer is going on. Thus to help the child leads him to depend on the teacher instead of relying on his own knowledge. It leads to guessing, and so skillful does this sometimes become that a bright but unprepared pupil is able to steer through a recitation guided by the unsuspecting teacher.

Answers should not be repeated by the teacher. This is a very common fault, and a habit that is usually acquired before the teacher is aware of it. The tendency to repeat answers probably arises at first from a mental unreadiness on the part of the teacher. He has not his next question quite ready, and so bridges over the interval by saying over the answer just given by the pupil. It is a method of gaining time, but really finally results in great loss of time in the recitation. By actual count, many teachers have been found to repeat as many as 75% of the answers given in[78] the recitation. Besides the great waste of time, the repetition of answers is a source of distraction and annoyance to pupils. No one enjoys having his words said over after him constantly. Of course answers may sometimes need to be repeated to emphasize some important point. But when repetition has become a habit, no emphasis is gained by the repetition.

Finally, answers should be required in good English, clear and definite, like the questions. Pupils who say, "An improper fraction is 'where' the numerator is greater than the denominator"; "A compound sentence is 'when' it has two or more independent clauses," should be led to restate their answers in clear and correct language.

[81]

IV

CONDITIONS NECESSARY TO A GOOD RECITATION

We have now discussed the aim of the recitation, its methods, and the principles governing the art of questioning. But no matter how well defined the aim for the recitation, no matter how excellent its method, no matter how skilled the teacher may be in the art of questioning, these things alone cannot make a good recitation. Certain other fundamental conditions must obtain if the recitation is to be a success. Let us now discuss the more important of these conditions.

1. *Freedom from distractions*

Distractions of any nature result in a double waste. First, a waste of power through preventing concentration and continuity of thought. Try as hard as one may, he cannot secure the best results from his mental effort, if his stream[82] of thought is being broken in upon. The loss by this process is comparable to that involved in running a train of cars, stopping it every ten rods instead of every ten or every one hundred miles. But this form of waste is not all. There is also a serious waste of interest and enthusiasm resulting from interrupted recitations. Every teacher has at times felt the sudden drop in attention and interest on the part of the class after some interruption which took the minds of the class off the subject. Try as hard as the teacher may, it is impossible to go back to the same level of efficiency after such a break. The following show some of the chief sources of distractions: —

a. Distractions by the teacher. —Strange as it may seem, many teachers are to be criticised on this point. Any striking feature or peculiarity of manner, dress, or carriage which attracts the attention of the class is a distraction. A loud or ill-modulated voice, tones too low or indistinct to be heard well, the habit of walking up and down the aisles or back and forth before the class, assuming awkward positions standing or[83] sitting before the class—these are all personal factors which the teacher needs to keep constantly under surveillance.

The teacher may also distract the class by answering questions asked by the pupils at their seats, or by rebuking misdemeanors seen among those not in the recitation. Most of such interruptions are wholly unnecessary, and could be avoided by a little foresight and management. The lesson should be so clearly assigned that the pupils can have no excuse to ask later about the assignment, and then there should be a penalty for forgetting it. The drinks of water should be had and the errands attended to between classes. The pencils should be supplied and sharpened before the session begins. The mischievous culprits should be taught that it is a serious offense to interrupt a recitation. The teacher who permits these distractions by the school has not yet learned the secret of good management, and could hardly advertise his inefficiency in this regard any more effectively than by permitting such interruptions to continue.

It is also possible for the teacher to distract[84] the person reciting by interrupting when there is a slight pause to think of the next point, or a hesitation before pronouncing a word. Teachers sometimes even interrupt a pupil who is reciting and themselves offer explanations, make remarks, or continue the discussion, leaving the child standing and not knowing whether he is excused or not. Of course this is bad manners on the part of the teacher, and it is even worse pedagogy. It is not encouraging to the pupil to feel that he may be interrupted at any moment, and few can think clearly or recite well when expecting such interruptions. The pupil should not expect to be allowed to think out a lesson or a point when he is reciting, which he should have thought out before coming to class. On the other hand, the teacher must remember that the child's mind is working on what to him is new and difficult matter, and hence cannot move as rapidly as the teacher's.

b. Distractions by the class.—Inattention, restlessness, and mischief are great sources of distraction from the class themselves. All these things have a tendency to be contagious, and in[85] any case always break in upon the train of thought of the recitation. Because of this the teacher *must* win the inattentive and restless, and *must* check the restless, if he would save his recitation.

Not infrequently, in the more elementary classes, a certain kind of distraction is fostered and encouraged by the teacher with the aim of securing the attention of the whole class to the one who is reciting. This form of distraction consists in having the whole class watch the one who is reciting, and, if they observe an error in the recitation, at once raise their hands, when the one reciting must stop. This is a mistake from almost every standpoint, and has very little to redeem it. It may result in closer attention on the part of the class; but the motive which prompts the attention is bad. It leads to elation and rejoicing over the mistakes and failures of another, and it centres attention on the mistakes rather than on the facts to be brought out. Attention should be trained so that it will not have to depend on this kind of motive, and the memory should be trained to note and[86] hold a correction until the one reciting has finished. Further, it is a most serious distraction to the one who is reciting to be expecting that a forest of hands may at any moment be wildly waving about his ears, gleefully announcing that he has made an error. Condemnation of this method of securing attention can hardly be too severe.

c. Distractions by the school. — In any busy school there is bound to be more or less of hum and confusion. In many schools, however, there is much more than is warranted. It is true that children get tired of sitting still for an entire session, and that they find relief in going for a drink, or going to the dictionary, or on some other errand about the room. In some schools, one or more pupils may be found walking about the room at almost any time of the day, and not infrequently several are on errands at the same time. This, as previously noted, is usually a fault in management on the part of the teacher. The larger part of these interruptions can just as well be saved by a little foresight and firmness.

Some teachers even leave the class which they[87] are hearing to answer questions or give help to pupils in the school who have not been trained to wait for their requests until the class is dismissed. Usually, only a very small percentage of these questions should have been asked at all, or would have been with the proper management of the school. And all the necessary questions and requests should almost without exception be held for the interval between recitations. The school should be taught that nothing short of the direst necessity will warrant asking a question or making a request during a recitation.

Likewise in the case of misdemeanors. The class which is reciting should not be interrupted for minor misdemeanors which occur during the recitation. This does not mean that the misdemeanor is to go by unnoticed. On the contrary, the settlement for it may be all the more severe for having to wait until the class is dismissed.

d. Physical distractions. —Distractions from the physical environment may be of several kinds.

Not infrequently, especially in the older school[88]houses, the seats are so placed with reference to windows that the light strikes the eyes of the pupils, instead of the pages of the books; or it may be that a stray sunbeam strikes athwart the class and dazzles the eyes. It need hardly be suggested that no such distraction as this should go unremedied.

In the rural schools the recitation seats are often near the stove, where the temperature becomes unbearably hot when the stove must be generously fired to heat the remainder of the room. Not infrequently the ventilation is bad, and the room is filled with foul air, from which the major part of the oxygen has been exhausted. No matter how good the intentions of the class or how zealous the teacher, such conditions will kill the recitation.

Whatever may be the cause of physical discomfort or unrest should be remedied. One's body should be so comfortable and healthy that it does not attract attention to itself, except when needing food or other care, and it is the duty of the school to do all possible to bring this condition about.[89]

2. *Interest and enthusiasm*

Interest is the foundation of all mental activity. Its very nature is to lead to thought and action. Grown ardent, interest becomes enthusiasm, "without which," says Emerson, "nothing great was ever accomplished." On the other hand, the absence of interest leaves the pupil lifeless and inert mentally, his work a bore and achievement impossible. Interest is, therefore, a first consideration in the recitation.

Interest is contagious. No one ever saw an interested and enthusiastic teacher with a dull and lifeless class. Nor can interest and enthusiasm on the part of a class continue in the presence of a mechanical and lifeless teacher. The teacher is the model, and he sets the standard and pace for his class. Unconsciously the pupils come, under the influence of the teacher's personality, to reflect his type of mind and attitude toward the work of the school. The teacher's interest and vivacity in the recitation depend on many factors, some of which are largely under his own control.[90]

a. The teacher's command of the subject-matter of the recitation. — A teacher whose grasp of the lesson is doubtful, who does not feel sure that he is a master of all its points, who fears that questions may be asked that he cannot answer or points raised that he cannot explain, can hardly possess an attitude of true interest toward the recitation. His mind is too full of worry and strain and embarrassment. He lacks the sense of ease and freedom which comes from a feeling of mastery.

Command of the subject-matter of the recitation depends, *first* on the teacher's general mastery of the branch, and, *second*, on being freshly prepared upon it. It behooves every young teacher, therefore, to strive for mastery as he teaches.

But no matter how good the preliminary preparation, this cannot take the place of the fresh daily review, which gives the mind a new readiness and grasp on the subject. Let the teachers who feel that their recitations are slow and dull, seek the cause first of all in their own lack of preparation in one of the two lines mentioned.[91]

b. The teacher's attitude toward his work. — If the teacher looks upon teaching as a mechanical process; if he looks on the recitation as "hearing the class recite"; if he realizes nothing of the opportunities and responsibilities connected with teaching children, then he can command little interest and no enthusiasm. If, on the other hand, teaching is to the teacher a joy; if he loves to watch the minds of children unfold; if he rejoices in his opportunities and responsibilities as a teacher, then he is sure to develop an interest which will soon intensify with enthusiasm.

c. The teacher's health. — All have experienced the mental depression and lack of interest in things which comes from over-fatigue. The most interesting occupation palls on us when we are fagged, or when our vitality is low from derangement of health. A case of indigestion may sweep us out of our usual cheery mood into a mood of discouragement and pessimism. Frayed nerves and an ill-nourished or exhausted brain are fatal to enthusiasm.

Teaching is found to be a very trying occupa[92]tion on the general health, and particularly on the nervous system. Many girls break down or develop a chronic nervous trouble in a few years in the schoolroom. The combined work and worry prove too much for their strength; and not infrequently, also, the teacher who boards and carries a cold luncheon to school fails to secure the right kind of food. This is especially true in the rural schools. Farmers have enough to eat, but often the food suitable for men engaged in heavy manual labor is wholly unsuited for one who works with the brain and does not have a large amount of out-door exercise.

Nor do teachers always secure enough pure air. The air of schoolrooms is usually vitiated to such a degree that one on coming in from the out-door air can detect a foul odor. But the air of a room ceases to be fit to breathe long before an odor can be detected from its impurities.

These are some of the chief factors which are proving so fatal to the health of many of our teachers, and to interest and enthusiasm on the part of the teacher in his work. Both for the sake of his health and his work, every teacher[93] should seek to control these three factors as far as possible. Strain and worry and wear of nerves can be greatly lessened by careful planning of work, by good organization and careful management, and by exercise of the will to prohibit worry over matters large or small when worry will not help solve them. The teacher can in some degree determine what food he will eat, even if it means a change of boarding-place. And surely every teacher can control the supply of fresh air for the schoolroom and his bedroom, and this is perhaps the most important of all.

d. Experience. — The young teacher, without experience, may from sheer embarrassment and lack of mastery fail to show the enthusiasm which he feels, for embarrassment of any kind and enthusiasm do not thrive well together. But if the teacher is really fundamentally interested in his teaching, the enthusiasm will soon come. And better a thousand times the young teacher who is earnestly fighting for freedom and mastery in the recitation, than the old teacher who has grown wearied of the routine and has made out of the recitation a machine process.[94]

3. Well-mastered lessons

Probably the worst of all drawbacks to good recitations is poorly prepared lessons. One of the greatest criticisms to which our educational system is open is that teachers try to teach and pupils try to recite lessons which are badly or indifferently prepared by both. There is nothing more stupefying to the mind, or more fatal to interest in school work than the halting, stumbling, ineffective recitations heard in many schools. Teachers who try to teach lessons with which they are not thoroughly familiar are but blind leaders of the blind, and both they and their pupils are sure to fall into the ditch.

a. Preparation by the teacher.—The teacher is the key to the situation. If he himself lacks in preparation, he can neither lead nor compel his pupils to the preparation of their lessons. He sets the standard. A stream does not rise higher than its source.

The teacher's preparation has two different aspects: (1) The general fundamental knowledge of the subject as a whole obtained by previous[95] study; and (2) the daily preparation by study, thought, or reading for the recitation.

In general it is safe to say that teachers enter upon their vocation without sufficient education. Our certificate requirements are low, and many enter upon teaching with little or no more schooling than that obtained in the schools where they begin teaching. Of course this is radically wrong, but it is the fault of our school system and not of the teacher. It behooves teachers entering upon their work with this scanty preparation to recognize their limitations, however, and to do their best to remedy them. Low grade of certificate, low standings in any branches, or the teacher's own consciousness of lack of mastery should be sufficient to send the sincere and earnest teacher to school again, even if this must be to summer schools instead of longer sessions. This sacrifice will not only pay abundantly in higher salary, but also in greater teaching power and in the sense of greater mastery and personal growth.

But no amount of preparation in a branch will relieve a teacher of the necessity of daily preparation for the recitation. Dr. Arnold expressed this[96] thought when he said: "I prefer that my pupils shall drink from a running stream, rather than from a stagnant pool." In order that one may develop a line of thought easily it must be *fresh* in his mind; it is not enough that he has once known it well. One of the master teachers of our country, a university professor who is recognized as a great authority in his chosen subject, Latin, recently said to a group of Latin teachers: "I have taught Cicero for twenty years, until I know it by heart. But yet, every day, one hour before the time for my Cicero class, I go to my study and spend an hour with Cicero, just to get into the spirit of it. I would not dare to meet my class without this."

It is true that the teacher with twenty classes a day cannot spend an hour on the preparation of each lesson. But most of the lessons will not require so much—sometimes the preparation will be the making of an outline or plan, sometimes reading the lesson over to freshen the mind upon it, sometimes only thinking the lesson through, for its plan and topics. It may at times, however, mean hard and serious study to master[97] the difficult points and their presentation. But whatever it means, the conscientious and growing teacher will go to the lesson prepared to teach it in such a way as to inspire to high standards and mastery on the part of the pupils.

b. Preparation by the class.—But in addition to the well-prepared teacher, there must also be a well-prepared class. The teacher cannot make bricks without straw. Every failure to recite when called upon is a dead weight upon the progress of the recitation; and each failure makes it easier for the next one to fail with impunity, or at least without disgrace. It therefore behooves the teacher who would have inspiring recitations to lead the pupils to a high standard of preparation.

The pupil's preparation of the lesson should include two distinct lines: (1) Mastery of the facts, thought, or meaning of the lesson; and (2) thought or plans how best to express the lesson in the recitation. Most pupils think they "have their lesson" when they have memorized it or come to understand it. They must also be made to see that an important part of their preparation[98] lies in *the ability to tell well what they have learned.*

4. *High standards in the recitation*

There is no more potent force than public opinion to compel to high achievement or restrain from unworthy acts. A school in which the standards of preparation and recitation are low presents a difficult problem for the teacher in the recitation. In some schools pupils who are diffident about reciting, or who do not care to take the trouble, shake their heads in refusal almost before they hear the question in full. Others sit in stolid silence when called upon, and make no response of any kind. In still other cases the class smile or giggle when several have been called upon and have failed to recite, thus taking the failure as a joke.

Of course such a lack of standards proclaims the previous teaching to have been weak and bungling. It shows the effects of a teacher without standards or skill. But the immediate question is how to remedy such an evil situation when one finds it existing in a school.[99]

It is probable that low standards come as often from work that is too difficult or too great in amount as from any other source. If the child fails to understand the lesson, or has not had time to master it, he cannot recite, however much he may desire to. All that is left for him is to decline when called upon. He may be chagrined at first over his failure; but if failure follows failure, he soon ceases to care when unable to recite. The remedy suggests itself at once; assign lessons that are within the child's ability, and also within the time available for their preparation. Then *insist that the work be done and the recitation be made.*

If the failure comes from laziness, lack of study, indulgence in mischief, or any such cause, the remedy will be a different one. But a remedy must be devised and applied. No school can run successfully without good standards well maintained for the recitation. The teacher who feels that the standards of the school are too low in this particular should never be satisfied until the cause for such a condition is discovered, and worthy standards instituted. This will be one of[100] the hardest tests upon the teacher's ingenuity and skill.

The public opinion of the school must be brought to take the recitation seriously. It must not be a cause for levity when several pupils fail. Failure must come to be looked forward to with apprehension, and looked back upon with humiliation. And all this must be done without scolding and bickering. It must be done with great patience and good nature, but it must be done. The teacher must himself have a high standard of excellence, and must persistently impress this upon his class. Here again the ideals of the teacher are contagious.

5. *A spirit of coöperation*

Much depends on the spirit with which class and teacher enter upon the recitation. If the spirit of coöperation is lacking; if the relations between teacher and pupils are strained or not cordial; if the class look upon the recitation as a kind of game in which the teacher tries to corner and catch the class, and the class try to avoid being cornered and caught, then the recitation is certain to be a failure.[101]

Under skillful teaching the pupils should come to look forward to the recitation with pleasure and anticipation. It should be a time when teacher and class work together in whole-hearted, enthusiastic effort, with the common aim of bringing the class to master more fully the matter of the lesson. There should be no feeling that the teacher has one aim and the class another aim, or that their interests are in any way antagonistic; no feeling that the teacher's highest ambition is to catch pupils in errors, and the pupil's highest achievement to avoid being caught. There should be no attempt at bluffing, or covering up errors or points not understood.

Probably the greatest factor in establishing and maintaining a spirit of coöperation between teacher and class is a deep-seated and sympathetic desire on the part of the teacher to be helpful. If his attitude is that of a friend and co-worker, and his criticisms and corrections are all made in the spirit of helping to a better understanding rather than in the spirit of fault-finding, this will go far toward establishing a spirit of coöperation in the class.[102]

This does not mean that the teacher shall be weak, and let mistakes or failures go by unnoticed. Weak teachers are never liked or respected. It only means that the teacher, in making corrections or calling attention to failures, shall manifest the spirit of a helper and not of a faultfinder. It means that no matter how many times a teacher may have to correct or even punish a pupil, his attitude toward the pupil will still be cordial and friendly. There are many persons who cannot correct a fault without having some enmity arise toward the one corrected. But what the teacher needs is to be able to correct, rebuke or punish, and at the same time keep the heart warm toward the wrongdoer. This will not only secure better results from the corrections, but will also foster the spirit of helpfulness and coöperation between teacher and school.

Finally, the class should be brought to see that the school is *their* school, and not the teacher's school or the board's school. They should realize that failure or low achievement is their loss, and not the teacher's loss. They should feel that their interests and those of the teacher, the board,[103] and the taxpayers who support the school are all *common interests*, and that only as the pupils do their part will the interests of all be conserved.

[107]

V

THE ASSIGNMENT OF THE LESSON

1. *The importance of proper assignment*

Upon the proper assignment of the lesson depends much of the success of the recitation, and also much of the pupils' progress in learning how to study. The assignment of the lesson thus becomes one of the most important duties of the recitation period. Too many times this is left until the very close of the class hour, when there is no time left for proper assignment, and the teacher can only say, "Take the next four pages," or "Work out the next twenty problems."

2. *Good assignment and teaching the art of study*

We forget that children do not understand how to go to work at the lesson as we know how. The result is that they come back to the[108] next recitation listless and uninterested, with the lesson not prepared. Or, it may happen that the less timid ones, when they come to study the lesson, call upon the teacher to show them how to go to work. The teacher has then to take time needed for other things to show different individuals what should have been presented to the entire class when the lesson was assigned. Such a method is comparable with giving a set of tools into the hands of novices who do not know how to use them, and then, without any instruction in the use of the tools, expecting them to turn out good work, without loss of time.

Little children are unfamiliar with books,—with the paragraphs, outlines, divisions, and subdivisions of a subject. They hardly know how to "gather thought" from a printed page, and yet we expect them to "get their lesson" without being shown how to go at it. Much time is lost in this way, and many children are discouraged in their work and caused to dislike going to school.

The Germans far excel us in this feature of[109] their school work. No class of German children are ever sent to their seats with the simple direction to take so many pages in advance. Teacher and class together go over the next lesson, the teacher calling the attention of the class to the points of the lesson, asking them to hunt out subdivisions, etc., and instructing them how to prepare the lesson. And the class, having this necessary help, are able to prepare their lesson better and recite it better than the American children of the same age.

3. *The teacher's preparation for assignment*

There are three chief reasons why teachers do not give more attention to the assignment of the lesson: (1) Lack of time, (2) failure themselves to prepare the lesson in advance so as to be able to assign it, and (3) lack of understanding of proper methods of study.

Lack of time is not an adequate excuse for failure properly to assign the lesson. If there is but fifteen minutes for the recitation, all the more reason why this time should be used to the best advantage for the pupils. If one third of this[110] time should be taken for the assignment of the next lesson (and this is usually not too large a proportion in elementary classes), then this much time should be taken. And, besides, if the lesson is well assigned, so that it is better understood and prepared by the class, more can be accomplished in ten minutes of actual reciting than in fifteen under the old method.

It may sometimes be advisable to assign the advance lesson at the beginning of the recitation, but usually it is better to wait until the close; for then the connection between the present lesson and the next can better be brought out.

Failure to look ahead in the textbook and become familiar with the next lesson renders it impossible properly to make the assignment. The teacher must know the scope of the lesson, its chief points, and the main difficulties it will present to the class. How often teachers are obliged to say to an unprepared class: "I did not realize how hard that lesson was, or I would not have assigned so much"; or, "That lesson was longer than I intended." All of which is a confession that the teacher was unprepared to make[111] the assignment properly. It is true that the teacher is very busy and has many lessons to prepare; but, on the other hand, the teacher who keeps a day ahead of the class in his preparation will find that it abundantly pays in the greater mastery of his subject and the time saved in reviewing it preparatory to the recitation. This is not time lost, it is time saved.

The young teacher's lack of knowledge of the principles underlying the art of study is a more serious matter, and a difficulty harder to overcome. Every teacher should make a special study of the psychology of attention and interest. He should also come to know how the mind naturally approaches any new subject, first securing a *synthetic* or bird's-eye view of it as a whole; how next it *analyzes* it into its elements; and how finally it thinks them together, or *synthesizes* them, into a new and better-understood whole.

4. *How to assign a lesson*

There may, of course, be some lessons that can properly be assigned in a moment by telling the class how much to take in advance. This is[112] true of lessons that are only a continuation of matter with which the class are already somewhat familiar, which they know how to study, and which contains no special difficulties. For example, spelling lessons presenting no new difficulties or especially hard words; arithmetic lessons containing practice problems intended for drill, but no new topics for study; grammar lessons consisting of applications of principles or rules already mastered. But all lessons that are built upon a logical outline, or contain new or difficult principles, or involve especial difficulties of any kind should be assigned carefully and with sufficient detail to make sure that the class know how to go to work in preparing the lesson without loss of time and interest.

It is necessary, however, to observe a caution in this connection. There is some danger of assigning lessons in such a way as to render too much help, and thus relieve the pupil of the necessity of mastering it for himself. It is difficult to say whether the mistake of helping too much in the assignment, or not helping enough is the more serious. The teacher must know his class[113] and his text-book, and then use the best judgment he has in making just such suggestions as will result in the best effort and mastery by the pupils without robbing them of the necessity for work.

5. *Principles governing the assignment*

The following are the chief points to be observed in assigning the lesson: —

1. Go over the lesson with the class in such a way as to give them a *bird's-eye view* of the whole, a general idea of what the entire lesson is about, or what it is meant to teach. Sometimes this can best be done with the books open in the hands of the pupils, the teacher calling attention to the topics treated. Occasionally the teacher may himself state the aim or scope of the lesson without the use of the text. Getting this synthetic view of the lesson enables the pupil to begin study with better intelligence, and also helps him better to understand the relation of the separate parts to the lesson as a whole. In this bird's-eye view of the lesson its relation to the lesson just recited, or other previous lessons,[114] should be brought out so as to unite the separate lessons into a continuous view of the subject.

2. Suggestions should be given as to the analysis of the lesson into its different topics. If the text uses a system of numerals in designating the points, the pupils should form the habit of using these in studying the lesson. For example, finding I, they should look for II, III, etc., thus getting the main heads. Under these main topic numerals will often be found a series of paragraphs numbered 1, 2, 3, etc., indicating the different topics under each head. The system may even extend to sub-topics lettered *a, b, c,* etc. The pupil should early learn to look for and make use of these helps in the analysis of the lesson. And even when the author does not introduce any such

system of numbering he still follows some outline more or less logically arranged. No better training in analysis, and no better method of mastering a lesson can be found than for the pupil himself to make a written outline of the lesson, using such a system of numbering the topics and sub-topics as that suggested above.

3. Children should be taught to make a final[115] summary, or synthesis, of the lesson after they have analyzed it into its separate points. Of course a large proportion of the details learned and recited in any lesson will finally be forgotten. But this does not mean that such details were unnecessary. It rather means that their part was to help in bringing out the few main facts or points and making them clear. For most lessons can be reduced to a few chief points. These are the ones to be remembered and used in further learning. It is these important points which the pupil should summarize and fix in his memory and understanding as the final act in preparing the lesson. Not to do this is to fail to reap the best results from the work put upon the lesson, for these more important points are lost almost as readily as the less important details unless they are emphasized in some such way as has been suggested.

It is of course not meant that this summary of points should be worked out by the teacher when the lesson is being assigned. That is for the pupils to do as a result of their analysis of the lesson. But the teacher should specifically call at[116]tention to the necessity for such a summary until the habit is so fixed that the pupils follow this method of study without further direction. The pupil's summary of the lesson should be tested in the recitation just as much as his analysis of the facts of the lesson. This is done by few teachers.

4. Particularly difficult points, or points of importance as a basis for later work, should be especially emphasized in the assignment of the lesson. This will go far toward saving the fatal weakness on fundamental points which is shown in later work by so many pupils. Not having been over the ground before and therefore not realizing the importance or difficulty of the critical points in a subject, the pupils must of necessity be largely dependent on the teacher for such suggestions.

5. Pupils need to be taught to look up and come to understand the allusions and various references often used in history, reading, or

other lessons. The younger pupils will often have to be shown how to do this. Therefore such points should be referred to in making the assignment, and any necessary directions should be given.[117]

6. Not infrequently new or unusual words or phrases are encountered by pupils in preparing their lessons, and they are hampered in their study by failing to understand the new terms. The teacher, knowing his pupils, should be able to anticipate any trouble of this kind, and give such explanations or help as may be necessary when assigning the lesson.

7. In case written work is to constitute a part of the preparation, the directions governing what is to be done should be so clear and explicit that there is no possibility of their not being understood, and the teacher's being interrupted next day to explain to members of the class. Much time can be saved for both teacher and pupils, and many distractions prevented from disturbing recitations if this simple direction is followed.

8. If the principles suggested above are followed in assigning lessons, there will be little excuse for a pupil's forgetting the assignment. It will therefore be a safe rule not to repeat assignments for the benefit of careless or inattentive pupils. The teacher who will refuse to be interrupted during recitation hours to tell pupils[118] what the lesson is, but who will reassign the lesson for the pupil at recess-time, or after school, will very soon find all such troubles vanish, and will at the same time be giving his pupils valuable and necessary training in attention and memory.

[119]

OUTLINE

I. THE PURPOSES OF THE RECITATION

- 1. The teacher and the recitation, 2
- 2. The necessity of having a clear aim, 3
- 3. Testing as an aim in the recitation, 5
- *a.* The preparation of the lesson assigned, 6
- *b.* The pupil's knowledge and his methods of study, 7
- *c.* The pupil's points of failure and the cause thereof, 10
- 4. Teaching as an aim in the recitation, 12
- *a.* Give the child an opportunity for self-expression, 13
- *b.* Give help on difficult points, 15
- *c.* Bring in new points supplementing the text, 16
- *d.* Inspire the pupils to better efforts and higher ideals, 17
- *e.* Lead pupils into good habits of study, 17
- 5. Drill as an aim in the recitation, 19
- *a.* Drill should be employed wherever a high degree of skill is required, 21
- *b.* Drill must be upon correct models, and with alert interest and attention, 21
- *c.* Drill must not stop short of a reasonable degree of efficiency, or skill, 23
- *d.* Drill must be governed by definite aims, 23
- 6. A desirable balance among the three aims, 25

II. THE METHOD OF THE RECITATION

- 1. Method varies with aim, 29
- 2. Fundamental principles of method, 30[120]
- a. Interest is the first requisite for attention and all mental activity, 30
- b. The natural mode of learning is to proceed from the known to the related unknown, 31
- 3. The use of special forms of method, 32
- 4. The question-and-answer method, 33

- *a.* When and where to employ the question-and-answer method, 34
- *b.* Dangers of the question-and-answer method, 38
- 5. The topical method, 40
- *a.* Where the topical method is most serviceable, 41
- *b.* The question of standards in topical recitations, 44
- 6. The lecture, or supplemental, method, 45
- *a.* How the lecture method is to be used, 46
- *b.* Dangers from the lecture method, 47
- 7. The written recitation, 48
- *a.* The use of the written recitation, 48
- *b.* Dangers in the use of the written method, 49

- **III. THE ART OF QUESTIONING**

- 1. The importance of good questioning, 55
- 2. Need of fundamental principles, 56
- 3. The principle of freedom from textbooks, 56
- 4. The principle of unity or continuity in questions, 61
- 5. The principle of clearness, 64
- *a.* Freedom from ambiguity or obscurity of wording, 65
- *b.* Adaptation to the age and understanding of the child, 66
- *c.* Brevity, 67
- 6. The principle of definiteness, 68[121]
- 7. Secondary principles of good questioning, 73
- 8. The treatment of answers, 76

- **IV. CONDITIONS NECESSARY TO A GOOD RECITATION**

- 1. Freedom from distractions, 81
- *a.* Distractions by the teacher, 82
- *b.* Distractions by the class, 84
- *c.* Distractions by the school, 86
- *d.* Physical distractions, 87
- 2. Interest and enthusiasm, 89
- *a.* The teacher's command of the subject-matter of the recitation, 90

- *b.* The teacher's attitude toward his work, 91
- *c.* The teacher's health, 91
- *d.* Experience, 93
- 3. Well-mastered lessons, 94
- *a.* Preparation by the teacher, 94
- *b.* Preparation by the class, 97
- 4. High standards in the recitation, 98
- 5. A spirit of coöperation, 100

- **V. THE ASSIGNMENT OF THE LESSON**
- 1. The importance of proper assignment, 107
- 2. Good assignment and teaching the art of study, 107
- 3. The teacher's preparation for assignment, 109
- 4. How to assign a lesson, 111
- 5. Principles governing the assignment, 113

RIVERSIDE EDUCATIONAL MONOGRAPHS

Edited by HENRY SUZZALLO

- Andress's The Teaching of Hygiene in the Grades
- Atwood's The Theory and Practice of the Kindergarten
- Bailey's Art Education
- Betts's New Ideals In Rural Schools
- Betts's The Recitation
- Bloomfield's Vocational Guidance of Youth
- Cabot's Volunteer Help to the Schools
- Cole's Industrial Education in the Elementary School
- Cooley's Language Teaching in the Grades
- Cubberley's Changing Conceptions of Education
- Cubberley's The Improvement of Rural Schools
- Dewey's Interest and Effort in Education
- Dewey's Moral Principles in Education
- Dooley's The Education of the Ne'er-Do-Well
- Earhart's Teaching Children to Study
- Eliot's Education for Efficiency

- Eliot's Concrete and Practical In Modern Education
- Emerson's Education
- Evans's The Teaching of High School Mathematics
- Fairchild's The Teaching of Poetry in the High School
- Fiske's The Meaning of Infancy
- Freeman's The Teaching of Handwriting
- Haliburton and Smith's Teaching Poetry in the Grades
- Hartwell's The Teaching of History
- Haynes's Economics in the Secondary School
- Hill's The Teaching of Civics
- Horne's The Teacher as Artist
- Hyde's The Teacher's Philosophy
- Jenkins's Reading in the Primary Grades
- Judd's The Evolution of a Democratic School System
- Kendall and Stryker's History in the Elementary Grades
- Kilpatrick's The Montessori System Examined
- Leonard's English Composition as a Social Problem
- Lewis's Democracy's High School
- Maxwell's The Observation of Teaching
- Maxwell's The Selection of Textbooks
- Meredith's The Educational Bearings of Modern Psychology
- Palmer's Ethical and Moral Instruction in the Schools
- Palmer's Self-Cultivation in English
- Palmer's The Ideal Teacher
- Palmer's Trades and Professions
- Perry's Status of the Teacher
- Prosser's The Teacher and Old Age
- Russell's Economy in Secondary Education
- Smith's Establishing Industrial Schools
- Snedden's The Problem of Vocational Education
- Stockton's Project Work in Education
- Stratton's Developing Mental Power
- Suzzallo's The Teaching of Primary Arithmetic
- Suzzallo's The Teaching of Spelling
- Swift's Speech Defects in School Children

- Terman's The Teacher's Health
- Thorndike's Individuality
- Tuell's The Study of Nations
- Weeks's The People's School

RIVERSIDE TEXTBOOKS IN EDUCATION

- *General Educational Theory*
- Averill: Psychology for Normal Schools
- Freeman: Experimental Education
- Freeman: How Children Learn
- Freeman: The Psychology of the Common Branches
- Perry: Discipline as a School Problem
- Smith: An Introduction to Educational Sociology
- Thomas: Training for Effective Study
- Waddle: An Introduction to Child Psychology
- *History of Education*
- Cubberley: The History of Education
- Cubberley: A Brief History of Education
- Cubberley: Readings in the History of Education
- Cubberley: Public Education in the United States
- *Administration and Supervision of Schools*
- Ayres, Williams, Wood: Healthful Schools
- Cubberley: Public School Administration
- Cubberley: Rural Life and Education
- Hoag and Terman: Health Work in the Schools
- Monroe: Introduction to the Theory of Educational Measurements
- Monroe: Measuring the Results of Teaching
- Monroe, DeVoss, Kelly: Educational Tests and Measurements
- Nutt. The Supervision of Instruction
- Rugg: Statistical Methods Applied to Education
- Sears: Classroom Organization and Control
- Showalter: A Handbook for Rural School Officers
- Terman: The Hygiene of the School Child

- Terman: The Measurement of Intelligence
- Terman: The Intelligence of School Children

- ***Methods of Teaching***

- Bolenius: Teaching Literature in the Grammar Grades and High School
- Kendall, Mirick: How to Teach the Fundamental Subjects
- Kendall, Mirick: How to Teach the Special Subjects
- Stone: Silent and Oral Reading
- Trafton: The Teaching of Science in the Elementary School
- Woofter: Teaching in Rural Schools

- ***Secondary Education***

- Briggs: The Junior High School
- Inglis: Principles of Secondary Education
- Snedden: Problems of Secondary Education
- Thomas: The Teaching of English in the Secondary School

HOUGHTON MIFFLIN COMPANY